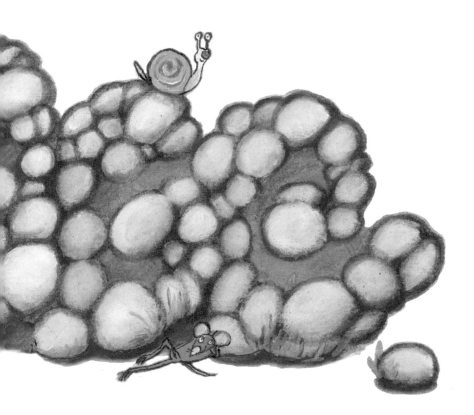

'Welcome!'
says our friend the Bird.

For Teuven,
and the Writers' Loft,
and the WDG in the alley,
and for everyone in the world.

and especially for Mother Nature...
'When I look into your eyes,
your love is there for me.'

George Harrison
It's All Too Much

————————————

————————————

contact Lisette Wansink:
www.wansinki-illustraties.be

Printed in Shenzhen, China

Publisher's Cataloging-in-Publication Data
Names: Ross, Warren K, 1953- author. | Wansink, Lisette, illustrator.
Title: Podge / Warren Ross ; Lisette Wansink, illustrator.
Description: Boston : Warren K. Ross, Jr., 2020. | Summary: Inspired by Mother Goose,
this collection of children's poetry offers silly rhymes and gentle philosophy.
Audience: Grades K-5.
Identifiers: ISBN 978-0-9903086-4-5 (hardcover)
Subjects: LCSH: Picture books for children. | Children's poetry. | CYAC: Stories in
rhyme. | Imagination--Fiction. | Nursery rhymes. | BISAC: JUVENILE FICTION /
Poetry. | JUVENILE FICTION / Nursery Rhymes. | JUVENILE FICTION / Stories in Verse.
Classification: LCC PZ7.1.R67 Po 2020 (print) |
LCC PZ7.1.R67 Po 2020 (ebook) | DDC[E]--dc23.

PODGE

A Podge is a Hodgeless Hodgepodge,
a pile of who knows what.

Why no Hodges? Well, not YET!
But we can get some soon, I bet.
Please, if you find a Hodge someplace,
it's welcome here — we'll make some space.

THE SHALL-WE'S

The Puddle

Shall we jump in the puddle?
Of course. We have no choice.
There it is, and here we are,
still smart enough to trust the voice
telling us that we must.

The Snails

Shall we walk in the garden,
and visit the patient snails?
Let's watch them wend
their gleaming slowpoke path,
and visit every friendly flower and fern.

The Button

Here's a button. What does it do?
Maybe we can guess.

It stokes the stars and the fireflies' glow
and raises the sun and sprinkles the snow,
and teaches the bees to help the flowers grow.

Someone pushed it long ago.
Shall we push it again?

And if we do,
what happens then?

Shall We Go a-Grimbling?

'Shall we go a-grimbling,
a-grimbling, a-grimbling?
Shall we go a-grimbling,
in the morning air?'

'That sounds like fun. What is it?'
'I thought you knew; I don't.'
'Well, if we don't know what it is,
then I suppose we won't.'

Whats for Breakfast

'What's in my pack?' said Peregrine Putz.
'They need a name! Let's call them Whats.
Whats for you and Whats for me,
Whats for breakfast and Whats for tea.'

The Which

The which went where,
just why we cannot say.

Which way the which went,
and with whom, and when,
and what they found there then,
we'll never know.

But someday,
maybe you and I can go.

Nostrils

How many nostrils should we have?
Two, it seems to be.
But if you want fourteen, or none,
or one on your nose and one on your knee,
or four on the floor and three in the tree,
my friend, that's fine with me.

Nkechi Nkele

Nkechi Nkele sat on a cloud
a thousand feet in the air.
But then I think somebody said
that really it was just her bed.

Maybe you are one of the few
who know that both of those are true.

Duchess von Bloop and her Hula Hoop

She never once used it, so they say,
and it rolled away one windy day.
Westward it rolled, to Foonimore Fen,
and soon it rolled right back again.

Flappington Flopp Makes a Mistake

Old Flopp, with a ticket for Floopston,
confusedly hopped off in Gloopston.
'Well then,' he said, 'What a ripping fine place!'
and paraded about with a smile on his face.

Blaine Wayne Forgets his Brain

Blaine Wayne is on that train,
but Blaine forgot to bring his brain.
Please find a brain for Blaine to borrow,
and bring it to Floopston by tomorrow.

MISHAPS of NO GREAT IMPORT

Special Elixir

Emily mixed a special elixir
from catnip and mandrake and tea.
It bubbled and boiled and then blew up,
and she landed on top of a tree.

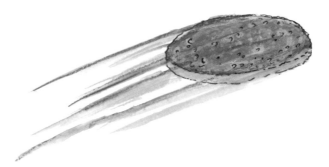

Flying Flapjack On The Loose

Apples, peaches, pears and plums,
look out Emily, here it comes.

Little Zack Zorner

Little Zack Zorner sat in a corner,
feasting on watercress.
He ate too much, then out it came,
and his Auntie cleaned up the mess.

THREE UNCLES and ONE ANT

Uncle Sprunkle Dunkle

Uncle Sprunkle Dunkle
sprinkles dinkles on his cat.
And then the cat runs off,
because the cat gets tired of that.

Uncle Nuncle Jackanapes

Uncle Nuncle Jackanapes
made a hat from a bunch of grapes.

I Know an Uncle

I know an uncle who rides an ant.
Don't say he doesn't, just 'cause YOU can't.

Little Crocus Crenshaw

Little Crocus Crenshaw
liked to bang and bash and crash.
She wrecked the world then flew to Mars,
to find new things to smash.

Lorelei Lila Farge

Into the town of Stroop one day
strode Lorelei Lila Farge.
And on her head she balanced a barge
as jaunty as a red beret.

'A barge, a barge, a barge!' she cried.
'And everyone who wants a ride
may climb aboard. Come, cruise all day
and dance and sing along the way!'

The barge all loaded, in she walked,
in depths above her nose.
And deeper still, she disappeared,
the silky silt between her toes,
and liked it there, and never rose.

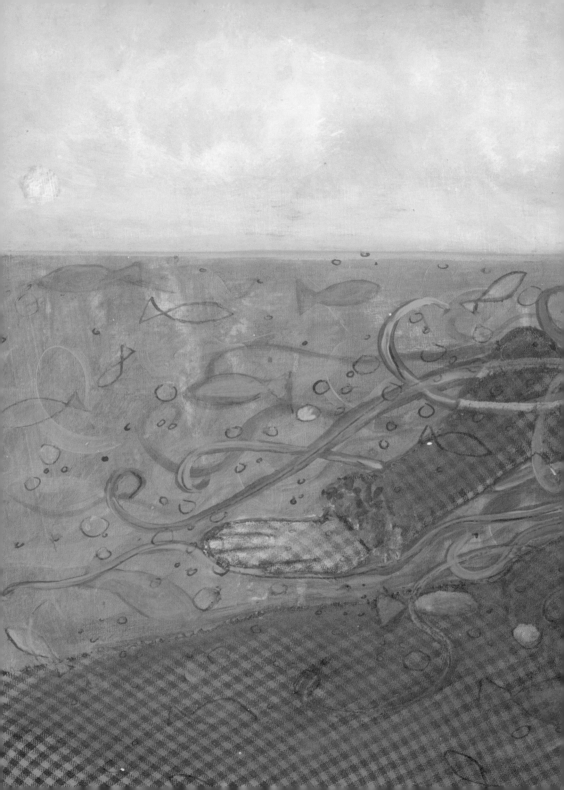

Bingwen Ding and the Flying Cake

For good behavior, Bingwen Ding
was given a cake by his mother.
He ate three bites, picked up the rest,
and threw it at his brother.

Hickory Dickory Hey

Hickory Dickory Hey,
I have some things to say.
You're nice. I like you. You're my friend.
Hickory Dickory Hey.

The Rocket Blossom

At four o'clock each fourth of June,
The Rocket Flower launches its bloom.
With a boom and a zoom this lavender plume
sets a course for the Drawing Room,
trailing a delicate fragrant fume,
to freshen the air for tea.

Schmilligan Schmulligan

Schmilligan Schmulligan married a mop.
They started to clean, and they'll never stop.

Marigold Pye

Marigold Pye wears a horse for a tie,
and sits with the world in her lap,
then thinks, 'My my, what an artist am I,
or something like that, perhaps.'

Gropius Gribble Houghton Huff

Gropius Gribble Houghton Huff
floats aloft like a milkweed fluff,
dropping blobs on the folks below.
Do they like this? I'd say no.

Plumpton Puckle

Plumpton Puckle went to town,
hoping his pants would not fall down.
His buckle was buckled nice and tight,
but something else was not quite right.

Here it Comes Again

Watch out Plumpton, behind your back,
here comes a Flying Flapjack Smack.

Spinka Pooka Polliwoggle

Spinka Pooka Polliwoggle,
rich from selling silver schnoggles,
built a zoo in Xanadu
and feeds her beasties Truffle Stew.

Delgado's Yacht

Something is wrong with Delgado's yacht;
just what, he couldn't say.
Maybe it might work better
if he tries a different way.

Blubbins McGlubbins

Blubbins McGlubbins launched from shore
in a sugar-pastry boat.
She didn't get too far. Why not?
'Cause pastries just won't float.

Dom, Dom, the Piper's Dog

Dom, Dom, the piper's dog
lived a week in a hollow log.
He didn't like it there, so then
he moved back into his house again.

Percival Schnook Learns to Cook

Percival Schnook, learning to cook,
made Fabergé Eggs with bacon.
The first time ever!
He thought himself clever,
then found he was mistaken.

Jarvis of Jabberly

Jarvis of Jabberly jabbered a lot
about things he did and things he bought.
And then one sunny April day,
Jarvis of Jabberly went away.

Unless You Live in Aldershot

Seven nothings aren't a lot
unless you live in Aldershot,
where nothing's something and something's not,
and things you haven't are things you've got.

The Foon Lagoon

Way deep in the depths of the Foon Lagoon
lives the Blithering Blobulous Blabberoon.
He talks too much but we don't care,
'cause we're up here and he's down there.

Pelican Peaslee

Pelican Peaslee sat in a tree,
with a duck and a cup of pumpkin tea.

Diddly Donkey Dumpkin

Diddly Donkey Dumpkin
made a home inside a pumpkin,
then diddled and dawdled the days away,
thinking of silly things to say.

Little Bo Peep

Little Bo Peep has lost her Jeep,
so now she cannot drive and beep.
'If I can't drive and beep,' she said,
'I'll waltz around and whistle instead.'

Old MacDonald Had a Farm

Old MacDonald had a farm
with critters that made no sound.
Folks would come and look a bit,
but never stuck around.

Then he heard the famous song
and knew exactly what was wrong.

Emmeline Hippleston Hoppleston Hyde

Sweet Emmeline Hippleston Hoppleston Hyde
lived a fine life and then she died.
If she had lived just half as long,
there'd be no need to change this song,

The Land Where the Scropalongs Roam

Parkie O'Clapp found an old secret map
of The Land Where the Scropalongs Roam.
He set out one day in his Anteater Sleigh,
and chauffeured them back to his home.

What fun!
But soon they were sad and sick
and stopped all their scropping along...

He said he was sorry, and then the next day
they all jumped into his Anteater Sleigh,
and laughed and sang and cheered all the way
to The Land Where the Scropalongs Roam.

The Missing Hodge

If your day is drab and drear,
get a Hodge and put it here,
right here on this very page
between this line and that one there.

And then you'll have, it's fair to say,
a proper Hodgy Podgy day.

Gurkle Burkle

Gurkle Burkle turned in a circle,
round and round, and then fell down.

The Purple Blurp

It came one day, the Purple Blurp,
a-knocking at my home,
or TRYING to knock — it made no sound —
'cause Blurps don't have no bones.

And now you ask, how could you know
the Blurp was there at all?
Did you SEE it at the door,
when it came to call?

No, I didn't see it,
but I would have, if I looked.
I had no time for looking,
I was much too busy cooking,
roasting ravioli
for my dinner guest, the Queen.

Nobblies on the Green

Nobblies on the Green,
Nobblies on the Green,
Nobblies on the Green, Franny,
Nobblies on the Green.

When will they be gone?
When will they be gone?
When will they be gone, Granny,
when will they be gone?

After they have left,
After they have left,
After they have left, Franny,
then they'll be gone.

Hodge-Podger

Rodger Zodger podges Hodges;
please don't say he doesn't.
I'd say it twice if it were true,
and never if it wasn't.

Rodger Zodger podges Hodges;
now I've said it twice.
So then, it's true, I hear you say —
unless I'm lying again today.

Rodger Zodger's Missing Podger

Rodger Zodger dropped his Podger,
and somehow it landed here.

He needs to get some podging done,
poking holes in hot cross buns,
and fill those butter-holes one by one,
and serve them hot to the Cobbler's son,
in the Village Square for tea.

I hope he finds his Podger in time;
now here's the end of another rhyme.

Doggly Woggly

Doggly woggly zoggly zed,
we brushed our teeth and went to bed.
The day is done for Podgers and cooks;
and we have finished this little book.

Thanks for Visiting

We made this book in our own way.
If you don't like it, that's OK.
We hope you make a book someday.
How about tomorrow?

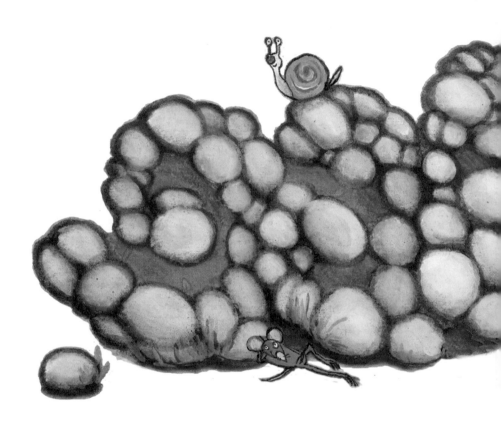